The Foolish Men of Agra

The Foolish Men of Agra

AND OTHER TALES OF MOGUL INDIA

RETOLD BY RINA SINGH • ILLUSTRATED BY FARIDA ZAMAN

For Amrita and especially Angad, my little Birbal

– R. S.

For Nanabhai and Gibran, and the two generations in between

– F. Z.

Canadian Cataloguing in Publication Data

Singh, Rina, 1955–
 The foolish men of Agra : and other tales of Mogul India

ISBN 1-55013-771-9

1. Akbar, Emperor of Hindustan, 1542–1605 – Legends.
2. Birbal, d. 1586 – Legends. 3. Legends – India.
I. Zaman, Farida. II. Title.

PS8587.I5583F66 1996   j398.2'095402   C96-930426-9
PZ8.1.S55Fo   1996

The publisher gratefully acknowledges the support of the Canada Council for the Arts and the Ontario Arts Council for its publishing program.

THE CANADA COUNCIL | LE CONSEIL DES ARTS
FOR THE ARTS | DU CANADA
SINCE 1957 | DEPUIS 1957

Key Porter kids
is an imprint of
Key Porter Books Limited
70 The Esplanade
Toronto, Ontario
Canada M5E 1R2

Distributed in the United States by Firefly Books

Printed and bound in Hong Kong, China by Book Art Inc., Toronto

98 99 00 01 02 6 5 4 3 2 1

CONTENTS

Introduction 6

The Reward 9

The Punishment 12

Birbal's Khitchri 14

The Eggplant 20

The Foolish Men of Agra 23

The Man Who Brought Bad Luck 28

The Journey to Heaven 33

List of Fools 38

Whatever Happens, Happens for the Best 41

The Never-Ending Story 44

Glossary 48

INTRODUCTION

FOR 181 YEARS, BETWEEN 1526 AND 1707, a magnificent empire flourished in India, as several Mogul emperors transformed a patchwork of small states into a great kingdom.

The first emperor, Babur, was both a scholar and a soldier. A Muslim descended from Ghengis Khan (the word *Mogul* comes from *Mongol*), Babur ruled his Hindu subjects tolerantly and became an inspiration to his descendants. Babur's son, Humayun, was weak and indecisive, and it was left to Humayun's son, Akbar – who appears in these stories – to consolidate the empire.

Akbar was drawn to mysticism and the arts, and he surrounded himself with interesting and talented people. His closest friend was Birbal, a clever Hindu courtier who rose to the position of state minister. The emperor delighted in Birbal's wit and wisdom, which inevitably made the other courtiers jealous. If popular accounts are to be believed, the rivals were forever plotting against Birbal. These plots, together with Birbal's wise counsel and humor, have a special place in these stories of the Mogul emperor and his minister.

The Reward

AKBAR WAS KNOWN THROUGHOUT THE kingdom for his love of the arts. His ministers had to make appointments, but artists could see the emperor anytime. Painters and sculptors, musicians and poets, singers and writers came from all over the kingdom to show Akbar their talents. And when their skills pleased him, Akbar rewarded them generously.

This infuriated one of the palace guards. Why should such ordinary people receive bags of gold and jewels for doing something of no use? Why shouldn't he be as handsomely paid? From that day on, anyone who did not offer him payment would not be allowed into the palace.

When Birbal was told that artists who could not afford to bribe the guard were turned away, he decided Akbar should know. He disguised himself as an old poet and shuffled to the palace gate.

"You can't go in," said the guard.

"I wish to see the emperor," explained Birbal. "The palace is always open to artists. That is known throughout the kingdom."

"The emperor is busy," said the guard, "but I might be persuaded to help."

"I have nothing to offer you," said Birbal.

"Then the emperor is busy," replied the guard, and turned away.

"I am confident that the emperor will like my poetry," said Birbal. "He will give me a handsome reward. Whatever I get, half will be yours."

The guard agreed and let Birbal into the palace.

Akbar was very pleased with the old man's poetry.

"What reward can repay such beautiful verses?" he wondered. "Ask for anything and it is yours."

Birbal bowed his head and said very humbly, "Jahanpanah, I will be content with a hundred lashes."

"A hundred lashes?" exclaimed the astonished emperor. "Why would you want to be whipped?"

But Birbal insisted, so Akbar ordered one of his ministers to give him his reward.

After the fiftieth lash, Birbal cried out, "Stop! Stop, Jahanpanah! I have promised half my reward to your guard."

Akbar was furious at his guard's dishonesty, and ordered that he be lashed and thrown in the dungeon.

And Birbal became even dearer to Akbar's heart.

The Punishment

ONE MORNING, AKBAR CAME TO court looking very cross. His mood seemed so disagreeable that his ministers and courtiers didn't dare speak. They quietly took their seats and waited.

Finally, one minister plucked up his courage and broke the uncomfortable silence. "Jahanpanah," he said, very respectfully. "You seem very disturbed this morning. May we ask what is the matter?"

After a very long pause, Akbar said solemnly, "Someone pulled my moustache."

The courtiers were stunned. Such an insult to the emperor was unheard of.

The ministers, relieved that Akbar was not angry with them, eagerly offered suggestions for punishment.

"Give the scoundrel a thousand lashes!"

"Banish him from the kingdom!"

"Throw him in the dungeon and starve him slowly!"

"That is too good for him. Stone him to death in public. Let everyone see the price of disrespect to our dear emperor."

While the courtiers shouted and argued, Birbal stood quietly, looking neither shocked nor angry.

"Why are you so quiet, Birbal?" Akbar asked. "Have you no opinion on this matter?"

"My opinion, Jahanpanah," answered Birbal, "is that the guilty person should be summoned immediately – and embraced in front of the whole court."

The ministers cried out in horror.

"This is an outrageous suggestion, Birbal," growled Akbar, looking furious. "Explain yourself."

"Jahanpanah," said Birbal. "Who would dare to touch your moustache but our little Prince Khurram? Should he not be hugged and kissed for such a beautiful crime?"

The sheepish courtiers could only look on as Akbar chuckled and smiled affectionately at his favorite minister.

Birbal's Khitchri

ONE WINTER MORNING, AKBAR, BIRBAL, and the courtiers took a walk by a lake, about a mile from the palace.

On their way they met a beggar. Upon seeing the emperor, he exclaimed, "Oh, Jahanpanah, ruler of the world, protector of the poor. May you live for a thousand years! Give a poor man a sikka – one sikka, Jahanpanah." And with that, he threw himself on the ground at Akbar's feet.

After handing the man a coin, Birbal mused, "People will do anything for money."

Akbar stepped into the icy lake to wash his feet. "I disagree, Birbal," he said, gasping at the coldness of the water. "Even if I were to offer a great sum, no one would stand in this icy lake for a whole night."

"I wish I could agree, Jahanpanah," replied Birbal, "but I know I could find someone who would win it."

"It's a challenge, then," laughed Akbar. "Find a person willing to stand in this lake all night, with nothing to warm him, and I will give him a hundred gold coins."

The next day, Birbal brought a brahmin to Akbar's court.

"I am a poor man, Jahanpanah," he said. "If standing in the lake for a night is the way to feed my family, I will do it."

"We'll see," said Akbar, and sent the brahmin to the lake with two

guards as witnesses.

The brahmin walked into the lake and stood shoulder deep in the icy water. At sunrise he staggered to shore, shaking so hard he could barely stand.

"Bring me to the emperor, please," he asked the guards. "The fortune is mine!"

By the time they reached the palace, the brahmin's shaking was no more than a shiver. "Jahanpanah," he declared proudly, "I stood in the lake all night, and now I have come to claim my reward."

As Akbar was about to hand over the coins, Abdul Karim, an ambitious courtier, saw an opportunity to impress the emperor.

"Tell us, brahmin," said Abdul Karim. "How did you spend the night?"

"In the water, huzur. I tell you the truth. These guards will tell you so," said the brahmin.

"And what did you do while your skinny body was freezing in the water?" asked Abdul Karim, contemptuously.

"I looked upon the palace lights glowing in the night," replied the brahmin.

"In other words, you cheated!" said Abdul Karim triumphantly. "You derived warmth from the palace lamplight. Therefore you have not earned the reward. Do not give it to him, Jahanpanah."

And the poor brahmin was escorted out of the palace.

A few days later, Birbal invited Akbar, Abdul Karim, and the courtiers for dinner. Many hours passed, but no food arrived.

"We are hungry, Birbal. Why are you keeping us waiting?" asked Akbar.

"The khitchri is taking a long time to cook," said Birbal.

"It is only a little rice with lentils. What's the matter?"

"Just a little longer," replied Birbal.

Two hours later, when there was still no sign of food, Akbar was becoming irritated. "Birbal, how long are we to wait for this meal of yours?"

"Why don't we see how it is coming along?" suggested Birbal, leading his guests to the courtyard, where a pot was suspended from a tree branch high above a small fire. Birbal fanned the fire, as if trying to speed up the cooking.

"What nonsense!" exclaimed Abdul Karim. "How can the heat of this fire reach the pot so far away?"

"It is not very far," said Birbal. "After all, the poor brahmin was warmed just by looking at lamplight a mile away!"

Akbar smiled. "You have made me see my folly, Birbal. The brahmin will be summoned first thing in the morning and given his reward twice over. But please, Birbal, may we have something to eat? We are very hungry."

"Dinner will be ready shortly," said Birbal, as he untied the pot and set it on the fire.

The Eggplant

ONE DAY, AKBAR AND BIRBAL were strolling through the palace gardens admiring the vegetables. When they reached the shiny purple eggplants, Akbar said, "Ah, the eggplant! The most delicious vegetable in the garden!"

"None can match its light, delicate taste, Jahanpanah," replied Birbal. "It is both handsome and nutritious."

Akbar was puzzled by Birbal's profuse flattery of the eggplant but couldn't figure out what he was up to.

A few days later, the royal cook prepared an eggplant curry, simmered with onions, ginger, and tomatoes, and flavored with coriander.

"Eggplant is such a bland vegetable," Akbar said, refusing the dish. "It is fattening and ugly. Serve it to Birbal. He is very fond of it."

But Birbal, too, refused the curry. "Eggplant is not only ugly, it is most difficult to digest," he said.

Akbar raised his eyebrows. "Birbal," he said, "the other day you were praising the eggplant. Have you changed your opinion so quickly?"

"Jahanpanah, the other day you praised the eggplant. Today you detest it, so I detest it, too. I am loyal to my emperor, not to a vegetable."

Akbar burst out laughing and called for a plateful of eggplant curry.

The Foolish Men of Agra

ALTHOUGH AKBAR ADMIRED BIRBAL'S WISDOM, every now and then it gave him great pleasure to test it, hoping to outwit his friend.

One day he said, "I have met with the wisest men in my kingdom. Now I wish to meet the greatest fools. Birbal, find me the six most foolish men in Agra. Bring them here tomorrow night."

"I will try, Jahanpanah," answered Birbal. "I will try."

The next morning, Birbal wandered through the streets of Agra, searching for fools. As he walked, he came upon a man lying on his back in a puddle of water, his arms stretched wide above his head, his legs waving in the air.

"What are you doing?" asked Birbal.

"I am trying to stand up. I slipped and fell in this puddle on my way to buy some fabric for my wife," said the man.

"Why not use your hands?" suggested Birbal.

"Oh no!" cried the man. "If I do that, I will lose the measurement of the fabric my wife wants."

"In that case, I will help you," said Birbal, yanking the man out of the puddle by his hair.

"Would you come with me, please?" asked Birbal.

"Of course!" agreed the man, too foolish to wonder why.

As the two walked along, Birbal saw a man riding a horse, with a bundle of straw on his head.

"Wouldn't you be more comfortable if you tied the straw to your saddle?" asked Birbal.

"I cannot do that, huzur," said the man. "My horse is so old and weak it might die from the extra burden. My own weight is enough for the poor creature."

"You are just the man I am looking for," said Birbal. "Please come with me."

"Of course!" agreed the man, too foolish to wonder why.

As the three walked along, they saw a man talking to himself. He was charging in their direction so fast that Birbal had no time to move out of his way, and they collided.

"Watch where you are going!" demanded Birbal.

"Watch where *you* are going!" retorted the man. "I was chasing the sound of my voice, and I was about to catch it when you got in my way!"

"Come with me," said Birbal. "I will help you find the sound of your voice."

As night fell, Birbal made his way toward the palace, with the three foolish men following him. Suddenly, near the palace gate, he noticed a man looking for something under a street light.

"What are you looking for?" Birbal asked.

"I have lost my gold ring in that patch of darkness," said the man, pointing to a spot some distance away.

"Then why are you looking for it under the light?" asked Birbal.

"How do you expect me to find it in the dark?" asked the man in return.

"Come along," said Birbal. "I will help you find your ring."

The man happily followed Birbal and the others through the palace gate.

"Jahanpanah!" said Birbal, as he lined up the men before Akbar. "I have brought you the four most foolish men of Agra."

"How did you decide they were the most foolish?" Akbar asked, amused by the strange group before him.

"By their actions, of course," said Birbal, and gave an account of each man.

"Well done, Birbal!" said Akbar, his eyes twinkling with mischief. "But I asked you to bring the *six* most foolish men. Here are only four."

"You have miscounted, Jahanpanah," said Birbal.

Akbar looked at Birbal very sternly.

"The other two foolish men are you and I." Birbal bowed respectfully. "You, Jahanpanah, because you set me such a foolish task. I, because I carried it out. That makes six, doesn't it?"

"It does, it does!" said Akbar, laughing until the tears rolled down his cheeks.

The Man Who Brought Bad Luck

IN AKBAR'S PALACE THERE WAS a sweeper named Gulshan, but everyone called him Manhoos, which means "the one whose face brings bad luck." People believed that if they looked at Gulshan, especially first thing in the morning, they would have a very bad day. They blamed Gulshan for all the bad luck in the palace.

In order to prove that such superstition was mere nonsense, Akbar ordered that Gulshan was to wake him up one morning and help him with his slippers. And he did. The emperor was very polite to Gulshan, who was extremely shy and rather nervous at being so near the emperor.

Soon after Gulshan left, an anxious servant came into Akbar's bedroom. Prince Khurram, he said, had a high fever. Akbar rushed to his grandson's side and hovered by his bed until the fever broke.

When Akbar returned to the court, a messenger was waiting. One of the royal inspectors was collecting bribes and illegal taxes from the poor peasants. Akbar dispatched a troop of twenty horsemen to escort the inspector to court.

All day long, Akbar heard nothing but complaints and bad news. Finally, he couldn't stand it anymore and marched off to bed early, in a very bad mood.

"What a day!" thought Akbar. "What they say about Gulshan must be right. He must be Manhoos."

The next morning, Akbar announced that Gulshan was definitely bad luck and would be hanged.

All the courtiers applauded, except for Birbal, who was extremely upset. He asked Akbar if he might question Gulshan in the emperor's presence. Akbar agreed, as long as Gulshan did not show his face at court until well into the afternoon.

"Tell me, Gulshan," asked Birbal, "what did you do first thing yesterday morning?"

"Huzur, I awakened the emperor," said Gulshan.

"And whose face did you see first thing yesterday morning?"

"Huzur, it was the emperor's face," answered Gulshan humbly.

Birbal turned to Akbar. "Jahanpanah," he said very respectfully. "You saw Gulshan's face first thing in the morning and you say you had a bad day. Look at this poor man! He saw your face first thing in the morning and he is going to be hanged. You are wise and just, Jahanpanah. You be the judge. Whose face brings worse luck – his or yours?"

"Birbal," Akbar said, "you are a true friend. You prevent your emperor from acting unwisely. Let Gulshan be set free."

Birbal said nothing, but bowed deeply.

The Journey to Heaven

SOME COURTIERS RESENTED AKBAR'S AFFECTION for Birbal, and the special attention the emperor paid him set many petty minds plotting. But Birbal was too clever for them, and time after time their schemes failed. Finally, in desperation, they hired the royal barber to rid them of Birbal.

"He poisons the emperor's mind against us," they explained to the barber. "Do away with Birbal and you will not have to do a day's work for the rest of your life."

Although the barber had nothing against Birbal, he was rather lazy; a comfortable life without work was tempting indeed. "Leave it to me," he told the courtiers.

The next day, as he shaved Akbar, he said, "Jahanpanah, do you know what your beloved father is doing in the next world?"

"What a strange question!" exclaimed Akbar. "How could I possibly know such a thing?"

"You could send someone to find out," suggested the barber.

Akbar laughed. "And how would I choose my messenger? He would have to die before his journey."

"Oh, no, Jahanpanah," said the barber. "There is an old magician who can send living people to the next world. He puts them on a funeral pyre, recites his secret spell, and they rise to heaven with the smoke."

"Can he bring them back?" asked Akbar.

"Very easily, Jahanpanah. He just reverses the spell." The barber paused, as if thinking very deeply. "However," he continued, "the journey to heaven is full of dangers, so your messenger must be very clever."

"And who would you recommend?" asked Akbar.

"None but the wisest and cleverest man in your kingdom," said the barber. "Birbal would be the best messenger."

"Aha!" thought Akbar. "Birbal's enemies are up to their old tricks. Let's see how he gets the better of them this time."

Pretending to be very pleased, Akbar smiled at the barber. "Of course, why didn't I think of him myself? Birbal is the perfect choice."

Birbal was summoned immediately, and Akbar told him of the barber's brilliant idea.

"Jahanpanah, this is an important journey," replied Birbal. "I must prepare for it carefully. I must also consider what gifts from our world would be appropriate for your father. It will take time."

"A month is plenty of time," said Akbar sternly. "One month from today you begin your journey."

Birbal bowed low and returned home. The next morning he began to dig, and soon a tunnel reached right from his house to the place where the pyre was being prepared. At the end of the tunnel, under the pyre, Birbal placed a metal door.

At the end of the month, Birbal reappeared at the palace, loaded down with gifts and weapons for his journey, and declared that he was ready to set out.

The barber and the courtiers had paid a poor old man to pretend to be the magician. He chanted some nonsense, gestured wildly, and lit the pyre. As the smoke thickened, Birbal slipped through the cleverly hidden door and crawled along the tunnel to his house.

A month passed and there was no sign of Birbal. Akbar was very disappointed in his friend and feared for his safety – perhaps this plot was beyond even his cleverest minister. Then, a few days later, to everyone's astonishment and Akbar's relief, Birbal appeared at the palace, dirty and bedraggled. His face was unshaven and his hair long and matted.

"Birbal! Thank God you are safe," exclaimed Akbar, hugging his minister. "Tell me, how is my dear father?"

"He is in excellent spirits, Jahanpanah," replied Birbal, "but he did have one request."

"No request of my father's could be denied."

"It is a small matter," said Birbal. "Not very important at all."

"What is it? Whatever he wishes he shall have."

"Jahanpanah," said Birbal apologetically, "I am ashamed to come before you looking so unkempt, but there are no barbers in heaven. Your father requested that, if it was not too much trouble, you send him a good barber."

"He shall have none but my personal barber," declared Akbar. "Pack your bags, barber! My father needs a shave."

The courtiers did not plot against Birbal again for a long, long time. As for the barber, no one knows how he fared on his journey to heaven.

List of Fools

"BIRBAL," SAID AKBAR ONE DAY, "I want you to make a list of all the fools in Agra. It is important that we know who they are."

Birbal took the emperor's orders very seriously, so each day he went about the streets of Agra looking for fools and writing down their names.

Without Birbal to talk to, Akbar became quite bored – until the day a merchant arrived at the palace. He had come all the way from Arabia and had horses of the finest breed. He had even brought one for the emperor to see.

Horses were Akbar's weakness. No matter how many he had in his stables, he was always eager to buy more. Akbar inspected the horse and was delighted. When he excitedly offered to buy it right away, the merchant said, "I have a hundred more such fine horses. But for the expense of transporting them, I would have brought them with me. Would you be interested in seeing them?"

"Certainly," replied Akbar. "I shall buy any that are as splendid as this one."

Akbar ordered the treasurer to give a thousand gold coins to the merchant to pay for bringing the horses from Arabia. The merchant bowed low and promised to return before the new moon.

When Birbal returned to the court, Akbar couldn't wait to show off his newest treasure.

"Look at him, Birbal," said the delighted emperor. "Is he not the most beautiful creature you have ever seen? What's more, the merchant is bringing a hundred more for me to choose from. And I gave him only a thousand gold coins as an advance."

"Only a thousand gold coins? So much money?" asked Birbal in disbelief.

"Why not?" asked Akbar. "It's a bargain."

"Jahanpanah, do you know this merchant's name? Do you know where he lives? Did he show you any references?"

"You worry too much, Birbal. Enough about the merchant," replied Akbar. "How is your list of fools coming along?"

"It's almost ready, Jahanpanah. Only one more name and it will be complete."

When Akbar unrolled the scroll, the first thing he saw was his own name.

"What nonsense is this, Birbal?" demanded Akbar. "Why have you put me on your list? And right at the top, too!"

"Jahanpanah," said Birbal most respectfully, "you have given a thousand gold coins to a perfect stranger. What can you call it but an act of utter foolishness?"

"The matter is not closed yet," retorted Akbar. "What if the merchant comes back, just as he promised?"

"In that case, I shall cross out your name," said Birbal, "and put in his instead."

Akbar laughed with delight at Birbal's wit.

Whatever Happens, Happens for the Best

WHILE OUT HUNTING ONE DAY, Akbar accidentally cut off the tip of his finger. "I am a fool, Birbal," he said. "How could I do something so stupid?"

Birbal wanted to console him but couldn't deny that Akbar had been very careless, so he merely said, "Jahanpanah, whatever happens, happens for the best."

Akbar had expected sympathy and was hurt by Birbal's inappropriate remark. By the next day he was both hurt and angry, for when the courtiers heard about his accident, their sympathy was unbounded.

"How painful it must have been," said a flatterer.

"I wish it had happened to me instead," said another, who was hoping for promotion.

Akbar's ministers quickly saw that this was an opportunity to poison the emperor's mind against Birbal.

"Forgive me for my boldness, Jahanpanah," said one delicately, "but you shower too much favor on that worthless man."

"He is getting too big for his shoes," added another.

"He should be taught a lesson," a third suggested. "Banish Birbal from the palace!"

Akbar agreed and sent a messenger to Birbal's house to inform him of his dismissal. In reply, Birbal wrote, "Whatever happens, happens for the best."

Many weeks passed, and although Akbar and Birbal missed each other, both were too proud to give in.

One day, while out hunting, Akbar became so intent on chasing a deer that he lost his way and found himself all alone. Suddenly, he was surrounded by tribal people of the jungle.

"Stranger, you are to be sacrificed to the goddess. She is pleased to receive human flesh," said their leader. "But first you must take a ritual bath – only a clean and perfect body is worthy of the goddess."

Akbar was outraged and told them he was an emperor.

They just laughed. "What kind of emperor is out in the jungle all by himself?"

Then he cried and begged for mercy, but they merely beat their drums and danced in a frenzy around the bathing pool.

Suddenly, one of the dancers noticed Akbar's damaged finger. "This man is incomplete! He is unworthy of the goddess!"

So, instead of being sacrificed, Akbar was escorted out of the jungle.

Back at the palace, Akbar could not sleep for thinking about his narrow escape. It was then that he realized that Birbal had been right. Had Akbar not lost his finger, he would have been a dead man.

The next morning he went to Birbal's house to apologize, but Birbal welcomed him warmly, as if nothing had happened. Akbar was delighted to be reunited with his friend, but one thing bothered him still.

"Tell me something, Birbal," he ventured. "You say that whatever happens, happens for the best. It is true for me, but how so for you? You were unfairly dismissed from the palace."

"Jahanpanah," said Birbal. "Had you not dismissed me, I would have accompanied you on your hunting trip. I would have followed you so closely that I, too, would have become lost. You were saved because your body is incomplete, but mine is whole, so I would have been sacrificed."

Akbar laughed and put his arm around his minister. "And now," he said, "it is for the best that you return with me to the palace."

The Never-Ending Story

ONCE, WHEN AKBAR FELL ILL, he found it difficult to sleep. Night after night he lay awake until dawn. The royal physicians prepared sleeping drafts and teas, ointments and medicinal vapors, but nothing helped.

One day, a wise old man suggested that the emperor's nerves might be calmed by a story; it was decided that every night one of the courtiers would take his turn at storytelling.

The courtiers dreaded this responsibility because, no matter how long the tale, Akbar was still wide awake at the end, asking, "And then what happened?" The storyteller then had to make up another story, and another, and another – and was always exhausted long before Akbar's curiosity. In desperation, the courtiers turned to Birbal and begged him to solve their problem.

When Birbal offered to be the storyteller that night, Akbar was delighted. What better way to endure insomnia than in the company of your favorite minister?

As Birbal finished his story, Akbar asked, "And then what happened?"

Birbal took a deep breath and began another tale. "Long ago," he said, "a hunter lived in a hut in the jungle. He knew how to protect himself from all the beasts, but the birds would fly into his hut and steal his rice. So the hunter went to town and bought a basket with a lid. He put

all his rice in the basket and shut the lid tightly."

"And then what happened?" asked Akbar eagerly.

"The birds befriended a mouse," Birbal continued, "and asked him to nibble a hole in the basket. When the mouse had done so, birds from all over the jungle lined up in front of the hut. Jahanpanah, do you know how many birds came?"

"How many?" asked Akbar.

"Five hundred," said Birbal.

"Five hundred! So many!" exclaimed the emperor. "And then what happened?"

"The first bird flew into the hut, stole a grain of rice, and flew away."

"And then what happened?" asked Akbar.

"The second bird flew into the hut, stole a grain of rice, and flew away."

"And then what happened?"

"The third bird flew in, stole a grain of rice, and flew away."

"Yes, yes. And then what happened?" asked Akbar, a bit irritated.

"The fourth bird flew in, stole —"

"Please, Birbal, enough birds have stolen rice in this story!"

"But, Jahanpanah," replied Birbal, "only four birds have flown away. There are still four hundred and ninety-six lined up in front of the hut. So, what was I saying? Ah, yes! The fifth bird flew in —"

"Birbal!" pleaded the emperor. "When are these birds going to be finished?"

"When you stop asking, 'And then what happened?'," said Birbal.

Akbar got the message, dismissed Birbal, and discovered he could sleep after all.

And so ends the never-ending story.

GLOSSARY

Agra a city in what is now northern India; the former capital of the Mogul Empire

Arabia an ancient area of the Middle East; now generally called Saudi Arabia

brahmin a Hindu of the caste traditionally assigned to the priesthood; named after the Hindu god Brahma

Hindu one who follows Hinduism, the dominant religion of India

huzur a polite form of addressing a man; akin to "sir"

Jahanpanah a term of respect meaning "protector of the world"

khitchri a dish made of rice and lentils

Manhoos a person who brings bad luck

Mogul an Indian Muslim descended from the Mongol conquerors

Mongol traditionally, an inhabitant of Mongolia, a country north of China

sikka an Indian coin